DONKEY KONG
COUNTRY

by Michael Teitelbaum

Interior Illustrations by Ron Zalme

Troll Associates

Also available from Troll Associates

DONKEY KONG COUNTRY: RUMBLE IN THE JUNGLE

Published by Troll Associates, an imprint and registered trademark of
Troll Communications L.L.C.

Printed in the United States of America.

10 9 8 7 6 5 4 3 2 1

Produced by Creative Media Applications, Inc.
Art direction by Fabia Wargin.

This book is dedicated to Matt's first year.

Special thanks to Roy Wandelmaier, Susan Simpson, and James Stepien.

One

The storm on Donkey Kong Island would not let up. Rain poured down in sheets. Thunder shook the tall trees, and lightning split the sky.

On the ground below his tree house, Donkey Kong stood talking to his little buddy, Diddy Kong.

"Sorry it's your turn to stand watch on such a miserable night, pal," said Donkey Kong.

"That's okay," replied Diddy. "It was just as bad last night when it was *your* turn to guard the bananas."

"We just can't afford to let our guard down with those Kremlings," Donkey Kong explained.

The Kremlings were evil creatures who had come to live on Donkey Kong Island. Their

factory polluted the island's air. And lately, they had been stealing food supplies from the island's many inhabitants.

"Don't worry about me," Diddy said. "I'll guard our bananas with my life! You can sleep soundly with Diddy Kong on patrol!"

"Thanks, kid," said Donkey Kong, giving his young friend a gentle pat on the head. "You're going to make me proud!"

Donkey Kong climbed up into his tree house. He curled up in bed, listening to the pounding rain and the wind lashing against his roof. He soon drifted off into a deep sleep.

In the stormy jungle below, Diddy Kong stood watch in front of the banana storehouse.

"I'm going to make Donkey Kong proud of me," Diddy repeated to himself.

Donkey Kong was Diddy's idol. He wanted to be just like the big monkey when he grew up. Diddy figured that standing guard against the Kremlings on a terrible stormy night was a good way to act like his hero.

Suddenly, Diddy heard a sound. It was not easy to hear over the noisy storm, but Diddy thought it sounded like footsteps in the jungle brush.

"Halt! Who goes there?" Diddy shouted. There was no reply.

A few moments passed. Then Diddy heard the sound again. *Footsteps,* he thought. *It's definitely footsteps!*

A knot formed in Diddy's stomach. His hands began to shake. "Stay calm," he said to himself. "Donkey Kong would be brave in this situation, and so *I'm* going to be brave too."

Diddy stood up straight and shouted in his loudest voice, "I am the brave Diddy Kong. Show yourself, if you are friendly. If you are not, then get ready for the fight of your life!"

Again Diddy got no answer.

He began to doubt himself. *Could I just be imagining the footsteps? Maybe it's nothing at all.*

Just as Diddy convinced himself that the footsteps were only in his imagination, a horde of Kremlings leapt from the bushes. "The fight of our lives, eh? Ha, ha, ha, ha!" cackled Klump, the leader of this group. "How foolish of Donkey Kong to leave his precious bananas guarded by a mere child."

"I'm no child!" yelled Diddy Kong. "I'm as tough as Donkey Kong, and I'll prove it."

"I'm afraid that is exactly what you are going to have to do, monkey," Klump said. Then he screamed, "Kremlings! Dispose of this pest!"

Two Kremlings raced at Diddy from opposite directions. He reacted quickly. Just as the Kremlings reached him, Diddy jumped straight up into the air. Diddy was a great jumper. In fact, he could jump higher and farther than even Donkey Kong. The two Kremlings crashed into each other right at the spot where Diddy had been standing.

Diddy came down on the head of another Kremling, startling the evil creature. "I told you Krem-bums I'm tough," shouted Diddy.

Meanwhile, a short distance away, Donkey Kong slept soundly in his tree house. The sounds of the struggle were drowned out by the noise of the raging storm.

Back at the banana storehouse, Diddy started his favorite move, the cartwheel attack. He sprang off his hands and spun feet-first into Klump.

The Kremling leader fell to the ground. Two more Kremlings dove at Diddy, who grabbed a vine and swung out of reach.

Diddy fought fiercely, giving the Kremlings a tough battle, but he was outnumbered. Finally, five Kremlings attacked Diddy at once, wrestling the squirming monkey to the ground.

The Kremlings stuffed Diddy into a barrel. Klump took the barrel and kicked it high into the air. "Have a nice trip, little monkey! Ha, ha, ha!" he laughed.

The barrel soared far across the jungle, landing with a *thud* in a patch of dense vegetation. Inside the barrel, Diddy Kong was knocked out.

"Quickly!" shouted Klump. "We have wasted too much time here already. That mini-monkey was more trouble than I expected. We must take the bananas and be gone!"

Two Kremlings lifted a huge tree trunk and ran toward the banana storehouse. Using the tree as a battering ram, they crashed through the storehouse's door, smashing it to bits.

As Klump stepped inside the storehouse, his scaly mouth began to water. Before him stood piles and piles of fresh ripe bananas.

"Hurry," shouted Klump. "Load the carts!"

The Kremlings took everything in the storehouse and piled it all onto their Kremling carts. Then they hurried out of the jungle, taking with them the Kongs' precious stash of bananas.

Two

B y the next morning, the storm had let up. Donkey Kong awakened to the gentle sounds of the jungle morning—birds calling, hippos splashing, and monkeys of all types chattering as they swung from vine to vine.

Donkey Kong yawned and stretched. "I'd better go see Diddy," he said to himself as he slipped out of bed. "I'm sure the little guy did just fine."

Donkey Kong climbed down from his tree house and made his way along the damp jungle floor. When he reached the banana storehouse, he stopped short. He stood before the smashed door in shock. Rushing in, he discovered that the Kongs' entire food supply was gone. There was no sign of Diddy Kong.

"Diddy!" shouted Donkey Kong. "Diddy, where are you? What happened?" His voice echoed through the jungle.

Donkey Kong was frantic. *The Kremlings must have staged a banana raid last night,* thought Donkey Kong, pacing back and forth. *Why didn't I take the watch last night? If anything has happened to Diddy, I'll never forgive myself.* "I've got to find him!" he said aloud.

"Find whom?" came a rough voice from behind Donkey Kong. "What in the name of monkey business is going on here?"

It was Cranky Kong, Donkey Kong's granddad. "Holy monkey madness, will you just look at that!" said Cranky. "Looks like the Kremlings made off with all our bananas!"

"Hi, Pops," said Donkey Kong.

"Don't you 'Hi, Pops' *me*," Cranky snapped. "Can't you ever do *anything* right? It's your responsibility to guard our bananas. That's the trouble with the younger generation today. No sense of responsibility. Why, in my day, we would—"

"Pops," interrupted Donkey Kong. "We don't have time for this now."

"Don't tell me what we have time for, whippersnapper," replied Cranky. "Why, when you were just a boy—"

"Pops, *listen*," Donkey Kong tried again. "Diddy was on guard last night. Now he's gone. The Kremlings must have taken him along with our bananas. I've got to save him!"

"Now, wait just a vine-swinging minute!" said Cranky Kong. "If you think I'm going to let you rush off on some dangerous adventure all alone, then you've got another thing coming! You'd probably just botch the whole mission, anyway. You need my experience if you're going to rescue Diddy and get our bananas back. Did I ever tell you about the time I single-handedly saved 14 gorillas from the—"

"*Pops!*" Donkey Kong cried impatiently.

"All right! All right!" Cranky said. "That's the trouble with youth, they're always in a hurry!"

Donkey Kong and Cranky Kong set off together on their mission to rescue Diddy and the stolen bananas. Donkey Kong brought a backpack filled with all types of special miniature barrels. These barrels had special properties that would be useful against any enemies. "I want to be prepared when we battle the Kremlings," he explained.

"That's the first smart thing you've said all day!" Cranky snorted.

Donkey Kong and Cranky Kong headed deep into the jungle. They followed the trail that had been left by the heavy wheels of the Kremling carts as they rolled away with the Kongs' bananas.

Suddenly, a barrel came rolling along from behind them. It struck both Donkey Kong and Cranky Kong on the backs of their legs, knocking them both off their feet.

"Whoa!" Donkey Kong shouted as he hit the ground.

"What in the name of monkey madness is the *big idea?*" yelled Cranky, landing with a groan.

Two Kremlings stepped out from behind a

large tree, laughing. "That's two dopey Kongs with one barrel!" smirked one of the Kremlings.

One of the Kremlings sprang on top of Donkey Kong. As Donkey Kong and the Kremling wrestled on the jungle floor, Cranky heard a tiny voice coming from the barrel. Then the other Kremling grabbed Cranky by the arms.

"Get your scaly hands off of me!" Cranky Kong shouted. But the Kremling just held him tightly and laughed.

Suddenly a huge four-legged beast came crashing through the dense jungle.

"Rambi!" exclaimed Donkey Kong, spotting his pal Rambi the Rhino as he pried the Kremling's fingers from his face.

Rambi was an immense rhinoceros with a giant head and an enormous horn. Rambi loved nothing more than smashing into Kremlings while running at top speed.

Rambi charged right at the Kremling on top of Donkey Kong. He bashed the Kremling, sending him flying across the jungle. At that, the Kremling who had grabbed Cranky released

the older monkey and began to run. Rambi charged and caught up with him a few seconds later, bashing *him* into the air and across the jungle too.

"Thanks, Rambi," Donkey Kong said, getting to his feet and brushing himself off.

"If there's anything I can't stand, it's Kremlings," said Rambi. "They're all over the jungle. Those two are the eighth and ninth Kremlings I've bashed today!"

"They gave us quite a surprise," Donkey Kong told him.

"Well, here's another surprise for you," said Cranky.

Right next to Cranky stood Diddy Kong!

Three

"**D**iddy!" exclaimed Donkey Kong, rushing over to his friend. "How did you get here? Are you all right?"

"I'm fine," Diddy Kong answered.

"I found him right in this barrel that the Kremlings rolled at us," explained Cranky.

"I'm sorry I let you down, Donkey," said Diddy, lowering his eyes. "I fought hard to save our bananas from the Kremlings, but there were just too many of them."

"You did your best, kid," said Donkey Kong. "After all, not everyone can be me!"

"Thank the maker of monkeys for *that*!" Cranky Kong exclaimed. "Now, are we going to stand around all day feeling sorry for ourselves? Or are we going to go get our bananas back?"

Cranky turned and continued into the jungle. The others followed.

"We'll get our bananas back, you'll see," Diddy said as they picked up the trail left by the Kremling carts. "Next time I meet those Kremlings, I'll hit them with a double-speed cartwheel. That will knock them off their feet!"

"I'm afraid getting your bananas back won't solve all the problems on the island," said Rambi, who now accompanied them on their journey through the jungle.

"You must be talking about the Kremling factory," said Donkey Kong. "I've heard about it, but have never seen it."

"Exactly," Rambi replied. "That horrible place is polluting all our air and soil. Soon no one will be able to grow any food or even breathe on this island. Something's got to be done about that factory."

Cranky Kong spoke up. "In my day, we didn't go around whining about our problems. We took action!"

"I've got some mini-TNT barrels with me,"

said Donkey Kong. "I say we go blow up that factory *and* get our bananas back."

"It won't be easy," said Rambi. "The factory is run by King K. Rool, the supreme leader of all the Kremlings. He's the biggest and meanest Kremling that ever lived. Even the other Kremlings fear him."

"It sounds like it's him or us, Donkey," said Diddy. "Otherwise, the island will get too polluted to live here anymore. I say we go for it!"

"I'm with the youngster!" Cranky said. "Let's give those Krem-bums a good old-fashioned monkey-barrel full of trouble!"

"It will be a long and dangerous journey," said Rambi. "We'll have to slip past the Treetop Village. It's been taken over by Kremlings, and they're ready to ambush anyone who goes past. I'll stay with you until we reach the edge of the jungle and help you get by there.

"Then you'll have to make it over the snowy mountains in order to reach the Kremlings' factory. You'll be running into enemies at every turn, and not just Kremlings. As I'm sure you know, there are plenty of other nasty creatures on the island. But if you're lucky, you may meet a friend or two along the way."

Diddy felt frightened. The thought of battling more Kremlings and who-knew-what-else made him wish he was back in his own comfortable tree house. He looked up at Donkey Kong, who smiled and patted Diddy on the head.

"You okay, little buddy?" Donkey Kong asked. "Are you ready for this adventure?"

"I'm ready for anything you are!" replied Diddy. Then he thought, *I can't let Donkey Kong know I'm scared. I've got to be as brave as he is!*

• • • • • •

The group moved on through the jungle. They soon reached the abandoned Treetop Village, with its wooden platforms and huts built high in a great tree. It had once been an active jungle community. But when the Kremlings began their assault on Donkey Kong Island, the original inhabitants had left, leaving Treetop Village deserted and dangerous.

"We've got to be quiet," whispered Rambi. "Move quickly and silently, and maybe we can slip past."

Treetop Village was also filthy. Its platforms and huts were now cracked and damaged. Garbage was thrown all around the jungle floor. The Kremlings simply tossed it down from the platforms above.

One by one, Rambi, Donkey Kong, Diddy Kong, and Cranky Kong tiptoed single file right under the village. Cranky lagged behind, moving slowly. He was moaning and complaining as he went.

"Will you just look at this mess?" he said as he stepped through the garbage, trying to keep his voice down, but not doing a good job of it. "These Kremlings are pigs!"

"Keep your voice down and hurry up, Pops," Donkey Kong whispered.

"Don't tell me to hurry up, whippersnapper!" yelled Cranky. "Why, I was walking these jungles before you were even—"

Donkey Kong, Diddy, and Rambi turned

toward Cranky. "Shhh!" they all said at once. But it was too late.

On the high platforms above, the Kremlings had heard Cranky shout. An alarm sounded, and Kremlings scrambled across the platforms, screaming at each other and loading their barrel cannons.

Donkey Kong heard several loud booms from above. "The Kremlings are firing their barrel cannons!" shouted Rambi. Donkey Kong looked up and saw a barrel hurtling right at them!

Four

Donkey Kong moved swiftly. He grabbed Cranky, pulling him out of the way. The barrel hit the ground, just missing the two Kongs.

The Kremlings continued firing their cannons at Rambi and the Kongs from the treetop platforms. Barrels rained down around them. Cranky ran for cover in the thick jungle growth. Rambi butted away any barrels that came near him with his big head.

Donkey Kong and Diddy used their best moves to avoid getting hit by the high-speed barrels. Donkey Kong ran, grabbed a vine, and swung out of the way of a swiftly moving barrel. Diddy jumped high into the air, then cartwheeled away from a barrel that narrowly missed him.

"I have an idea!" shouted Rambi. "Stand back!" The powerful rhino charged at the tree from which the Kremlings were firing their cannons. Rambi rammed into the base of the tree at top speed.

The huge tree shook from bottom to top. Kremlings came flying out of Treetop Village, crashing to the jungle floor.

"Let's give them a little taste of their own medicine," said Donkey Kong.

"I'm right with you, Donkey," Diddy Kong replied.

The two Kongs picked up the barrels that had been fired at them and furiously flung them back at the startled Kremlings.

"Here, catch!" Donkey Kong shouted as he threw a barrel with all his strength. The barrel knocked over three Kremlings at once.

"Nice shot!" said Diddy. He lifted a barrel to his chest and heaved it, flattening a Kremling who had just gotten to his feet.

The remaining Kremlings fled from Treetop Village in fear, now that they were unable to do battle from the safety of their perches.

"Cowards!" shouted Cranky, waving his walking stick at the retreating Kremlings. "Look at them run. Come back, you yellow-bellied lizards! I'll fight you one at a time!"

"Calm down, Pops," said Donkey Kong.

"Don't tell me to calm down!" snapped back Cranky. "I know how to deal with cowards. Why, when I was your age, I once fought five crocodiles single-handedly. I remember it was a day something like this. I had—"

"Pops!" Donkey Kong interrupted, rolling his eyes. "It's time to get going."

The group moved on and soon came to the edge of the jungle. Ahead of them stood a chain of tall snow-capped mountains.

"This is as far as I go," Rambi said. "You'll have to make it over those mountains in order to get to the Kremlings' factory. Be careful, and good luck."

"Thanks for all your help, Rambi," said Donkey Kong.

Rambi turned and galloped back into the jungle. The three Kongs were once again on their own.

The Kongs left the jungle and began their climb up the mountains. The higher they climbed, the colder it got. The ground grew slick with ice and snow. The traveling became more difficult, and Cranky complained more and more.

"Blasted baboon bottoms!" whined Cranky Kong. "This is a fine thing for an old monkey to be doing, slipping and sliding up the side of a treacherous mountain! This is about as bad as it can get!"

Without warning, a terrible blizzard struck. Driving wind and blinding snow whipped the Kongs as they struggled to continue their climb.

"So I was wrong," Cranky yelled. "It got worse!"

"What are we going to do?" asked Diddy, no longer able to hide the fear in his voice.

"I don't know," replied Donkey Kong. "I can't see two inches in front of my face!"

Suddenly a familiar voice called out from above, "Donkey Kong!" It was Donkey Kong's friend, Expresso the Ostrich.

"Expresso!" Donkey Kong yelled, trying to be heard over the wind. "What are you doing up here?"

"I was camping in the mountains," replied Expresso. "You guys look like you could you could use a hand. Actually, a foot. Well, really, *two* feet—wearing my sure-grip sneakers. Hang on. I'll drop down a rope."

Expresso lowered a long rope down the side of the mountain. Donkey Kong, Cranky, and Diddy all grabbed the rope, holding on for dear life.

"Hang on!" shouted Expresso. "Here we go!" Expresso's sure-grip sneakers gave him the traction the bare-footed monkeys just didn't have. The ostrich's powerful legs helped him pull the three Kongs up the mountain until they reached the ledge on which Expresso was standing. In front of them, in the side of the mountain, was the entrance to an ice cave.

"Let's duck into this cave," said Expresso when everyone was safely on the ledge. "It will get us out of the storm."

As they settled down for a rest, the Kongs thanked Expresso for saving them.

"What are you jungle folks doing up here in the mountains?" asked Expresso.

Donkey Kong explained about their mission to destroy the Kremlings' factory and recover their stolen bananas.

"Did you hear something?" asked Diddy Kong a few minutes later.

"Yes," said Expresso. "It sounded like wings flapping. And I know it wasn't *my* wings."

The flapping noise came again. Suddenly Necky and Mini-Necky, two evil vultures who lived in the ice caves, appeared. They began to take coconuts from their backpacks and throw them at Expresso and the Kongs!

Five

"**O**uch! Ooooch!" Cranky cried as coconuts bonked him on the head.

"Get out of our cave!" squawked Necky as he flung another coconut at Donkey Kong. "No jungle-dwellers are allowed in here!"

Donkey Kong reacted quickly. Dodging the flying coconut, he opened his backpack and pulled out two of the miniature barrel cannons that he had packed at the beginning of the trip.

"Here you go, Diddy," he called, tossing one of the cannons to his little pal. "It's time to play catch with these overgrown turkeys!"

Mini-Necky flung a coconut at Donkey Kong, who caught it in his barrel cannon. Donkey Kong fired the cannon, shooting the coconut right back at the vulture.

"Awwwk!" squealed the bird when the coconut struck him in the wing.

"I get the idea," said Diddy. He, too, began catching coconuts in his miniature barrel cannon and firing them back at the vultures.

"Let's go!" squawked Necky, who was not used to having his coconuts fired back in his direction. He and Mini-Necky flew out of the cave.

"Well, we took care of those guys," said Diddy Kong.

"We sure did," Donkey Kong said, smiling.

"If you two can stop congratulating yourselves for a second," said Cranky, "maybe you can tell me how we're going to get over these mountains to the Kremlings' factory."

Before they could answer, Expresso said, "Actually, you don't have to go over the mountains. You can go *through* them by using these caves and the old abandoned mines." Expresso pointed the monkeys in the right direction.

"Thanks for the rescue, Expresso," said Donkey Kong.

The ostrich nodded and then left the cave, heading back to his campsite. The Kongs proceeded deeper into the cave, walking along narrow, twisting passageways.

They soon came to a steep, slippery slope. The three monkeys stood at the edge of the slope, peering down into the darkness below.

"How in the vine-swinging jungle are we going to get down *there?*" Cranky Kong asked. "Not that I even *want* to go down there in the first place!"

"We have no choice," explained Donkey Kong. "We can't turn back, and this is the only way to go forward."

"Hey, Donkey!" Diddy called. "Look what I found!"

Next to a wall at the top of the slope stood a stack of old tires. "I bet we could ride down on these!" said Diddy Kong.

"I think you've got something there," Donkey Kong responded.

"I'll tell you what you've got," cried Cranky.

"You've got an idea that's about as bright as a burnt-out bulb!"

"Come on, Pops," said Donkey Kong. "It won't be so bad. Grab a tire, hop on, and hold tight!"

The Kongs each took a tire from the pile. They sat on the tires at the top of the slope.

"Here we go!" shouted Donkey Kong as he launched himself over the edge.

"Last one down is a Kremling!" yelled Diddy as he started sliding down the slope.

"Blasted baboon bottoms!" Cranky Kong cried as he pushed himself off. "I'm too old for *thiiiiiiiis!*"

The Kongs flew down the slope on their tires at high speed. "This is cool!" said Diddy, as the air rushed past his face.

At the bottom of the slope, the Kongs came skidding to a halt right in front of the entrance to the abandoned mines Expresso had told them to look for.

"What new horror do we have to go through now?" Cranky moaned as he shakily got off his tire.

The old mine tunnels were dark and damp. Donkey Kong led the way, feeling along the walls to guide himself. "Diddy, you hold my hand," said Donkey Kong. "Pops, you hang onto Diddy's tail so we stay together."

"Great," grumbled Cranky. "Walking through the dark on slippery rocks holding a little monkey's tail. Sounds like fun to me!"

As the Kongs made their way through the old mine tunnels, Donkey Kong spotted a light up ahead.

"What's that?" asked Diddy.

"I'm not sure," replied Donkey Kong as the light came toward them.

Squaaawwk! came a sound from the direction of the light. A few seconds later, a bright green parrot appeared, carrying a high-powered flashlight. "You folks look like you could use a little light," said the parrot. "I'm Squawks the Parrot. I live in the darkest level of this old mine."

Donkey Kong introduced his group and described their mission.

"You're in luck," said Squawks. "I know a shortcut through the mines that will lead you right to the Kremling factory. Follow me!"

Squawks led the way with his trusty flashlight, and the Kongs followed close behind. But as they came around a sharp bend, Squawks's light revealed Slippa the Snake and Army the Armadillo, two of Donkey Kong's cave-dwelling enemies.

"Thessse minesss are ourssss," hissed Slippa. Then he slithered forward to attack Diddy.

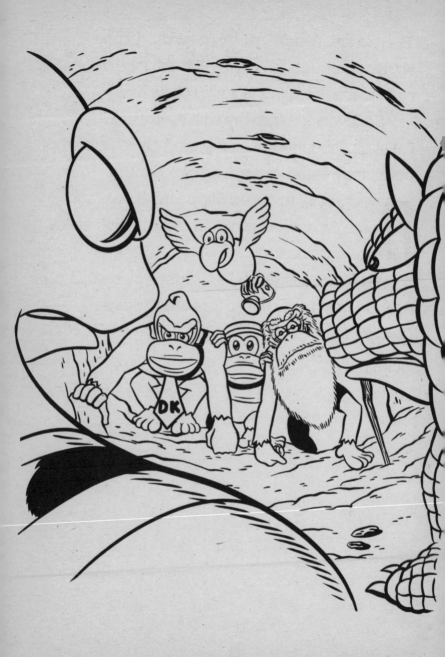

Six

iddy Kong reacted quickly, jumping into the air and landing on Slippa with his famous double-jump. The evil snake scurried back into the darkness.

Meanwhile, Donkey Kong pulled a barrel from the collection of special barrels in his backpack and heaved it at Army. The evil armadillo curled up into a ball to protect himself from the attack, but the force of the barrel knocked him far down the tunnel.

"Come on," said Squawks. "The shortcut is not far from here."

The group soon came to a set of tracks. On the tracks sat an old mining cart.

"The back entrance to the Kremlings' factory is at the other end of these tracks,"

Squawks explained. "Years ago, before the Kremlings took over the factory, the miners used to load their ore into the mining carts and then roll them right to the factory for processing.

"I think all three of you should fit into the cart. It may be a rough ride, but it will lead you right to the back door of the factory."

Donkey Kong and Diddy Kong climbed into the rickety old mining cart. Cranky stood next to it with his arms folded in disgust. "You don't actually expect me to get into that thing, do you?" he asked. "I've had more than enough wild rides for one day!"

"Come on, Pops," said Donkey Kong. "We've come *this* far."

"I'm going to regret this," groaned Cranky as he climbed in next to the others.

"Thanks for all your help, Squawks," said Donkey Kong.

"Yeah," grumbled Cranky Kong. "Thanks for helping us get killed!"

"Good luck at the factory," replied Squawks. Then he flew off.

Donkey Kong released the brake, and the cart rolled forward.

"*Whoooaaa!*" the Kongs shouted as the old cart sped up and bounced along the rickety old tracks. They plunged down steep drops and swung around sharp bends as if they were on a roller coaster that was out of control.

"If we ever get home," Cranky cried, "remind me never to get out of bed again!"

Soon the cart left the mine and came crashing to a halt. The three Kongs were thrown from the cart by the sudden stop and went tumbling over each other. They landed in a heap right at the back door to the Kremlings' factory.

"Is everyone all right?" asked Donkey Kong.

"Never been better!" moaned Cranky. "Of course, I may never walk again, but—"

"I'm okay," said Diddy. "And I'm ready to get those Kremlings!"

Donkey Kong examined the back door to the factory. It had not been used in so many years that the locks and hinges were rusted and broken. He gripped the door with his powerful hands and yanked with all his might. The old door came right off its hinges. "Let's go," he whispered. They slipped inside.

The Kremling factory was a dark, foul-smelling place. The sound of machinery filled the air, and the smell of fumes made the three monkeys cough.

"This is the junk they're putting into our air," said Donkey Kong. "Okay. Here's the plan. I brought enough TNT barrels to bring this whole place down. Diddy, you take some. Pops, you take a few more. We'll sneak around the factory, planting the TNT barrels every few feet. Then we'll meet back here."

Everyone agreed. Even Cranky went along without a fuss. The three Kongs were soon placing the highly explosive TNT barrels all around the factory.

When Donkey Kong was almost finished, he heard two voices coming from behind a large machine. He crouched down in a corner and listened.

"Where's King K. Rool?" asked a giant

bumblebee with big white eyes. "He's supposed to be at the factory *today,* Klap Trap."

"Well, he's not here, Zinger," replied a small Kremling with a long mouth and huge teeth. "He's the boss, so he can do what he likes."

"Just because this factory is his and he thought up the banana-stealing scheme doesn't mean he can ignore us," said Zinger.

"He's brought the bananas to his headquarters on the *Gangplank Galleon,* the Kremling ship," Klap Trap said. "He's at sea. We can't reach him even if we—" Klap Trap stopped short and turned in Donkey Kong's direction. "There's someone there!" he shouted.

Donkey Kong stood up to run, but Zinger buzzed him, missing his head by only inches. Klap Trap raced right at Donkey Kong. His mouth was open wide, revealing his sharp teeth.

From out of nowhere came Diddy Kong, cartwheeling at double speed. He spun right into Klap Trap, knocking him across the factory floor. Donkey Kong turned and slammed Zinger with his powerful hand-slap attack, stunning the giant bee.

"Thanks for the save, Diddy," said Donkey Kong.

"I was on my way back to meet you when I heard those guys talking," explained Diddy. "I saw them attack, so I came right over."

"Are all your TNT barrels planted?" Donkey Kong asked.

"Yes," replied Diddy. "Are yours?"

"All set," said Donkey Kong. "Now we just have to find Pops."

"I'm here, I'm here," said Cranky, walking up beside them. "What was all that commotion I heard?"

"I'll explain it later," Donkey Kong answered. "Come on. Let's get out of here."

The Kongs raced for the back door. When they were a safe distance from the factory, Donkey Kong detonated the TNT barrels by remote control. The terrible factory exploded in a huge ball of flame.

Seven

"**Y**ippee!" shouted Diddy Kong. "We got them. We destroyed the Kremlings' factory!"

"Don't celebrate yet," Donkey Kong said. He told them about the conversation between Klap Trap and Zinger. "We've still got to rescue our stolen bananas and find King K. Rool."

"So what do we do now?" asked Diddy.

"We head to the ocean and see if we can track down the *Gangplank Galleon*!" replied Donkey Kong.

"Great monkey madness!" cried Cranky. "I hate the ocean! Too much darned water, if you ask me!"

Donkey Kong shook his head. The three Kongs set out on the long trek to the sea.

• • • • • •

The following morning, Donkey Kong, Diddy, and Cranky stood at the shoreline, gazing out at the wide sea. Crystal blue waves gently rolled in and broke on the soft white sand.

"Now that we're here," began Cranky Kong, "did you stop to think that we don't have a *boat*?"

Before Donkey Kong could answer, a large blue swordfish broke the water's surface. His swordlike beak shimmered in the morning sun as he hung in the air for a second and then splashed back into the waves.

"It's my friend Enguarde the Swordfish," exclaimed Donkey Kong.

Again Enguarde jumped out of the water. "Dive in!" he called. "Don't worry, just dive in!" Then he fell back into the sea.

"I trust Enguarde," Donkey Kong told the others. "I'm sure it's safe. Come on! Let's dive in."

"Oh, great!" Cranky Kong moaned. "After all this, now I have to get wet!"

The Kongs waded out from the shore, then dove underwater. Enguarde was waiting, and he gave each Kong a special underwater breathing

barrel. Donkey Kong, Diddy, and Cranky slipped the special barrels around their necks and found that they could breathe and speak underwater.

Donkey Kong hopped on the swordfish's back and began to tell Enguarde about their adventures and their mission.

"I know all about it," said Enguarde. "Word of your adventures has spread all over the island. Even underwater. That's why I've been hanging around the shoreline, waiting for you. I figured you'd show up soon to find the Kremling ship.

"Grab onto my tail," Enguarde told Diddy Kong. "And you grab his tail," he continued to Cranky. "I'll pull you along as we go. I know where you can find that ship!"

Diddy Kong grabbed Enguarde's tail. Then Cranky took hold of Diddy's tail. Enguarde swam powerfully through the ocean, pulling his friends along.

Suddenly they were attacked by a gang of underwater enemies.

Chomps the Shark swam right at Diddy Kong. Enguarde rammed into the deadly shark with his powerful sword beak. "Take that, you overgrown guppy," shouted Enguarde as Chomps went spinning out of control.

Squidge the Jellyfish tried to sting Donkey Kong, who used a double hand-slap attack on either side of Squidge's head to stun the jellyfish. "That ringing in your head is not a phone call!" teased Donkey Kong.

Clambo the Clam spat pearls at Cranky Kong, but the old monkey remained unrattled. He used his walking stick like a baseball bat, hitting the pearls back at Clambo.

"Batter up!" yelled Cranky. "I wasn't the all-star hitter for the Kong Kardinals for nothing, you know!" Clambo swam away, stinging from the pearls Cranky had smacked back at him.

Croctopus the Octopus managed to grab Diddy Kong and Donkey Kong, but once again Enguarde and his sword were ready. "Get the point, Croctopus?" said Enguarde as he jabbed the octopus. Croctopus fled along with the others.

The Kongs regrouped with Enguarde, and they proceeded on the last leg of their undersea journey.

Enguarde and the Kongs surfaced. A short distance away, they saw the *Gangplank Galleon*. The large wooden ship bobbed on the waves. Up on the tall mast, a flag bearing a portrait of the Kremling leader, King K. Rool, flapped in the stiff ocean breeze.

"That's the ship," Donkey Kong exclaimed. "That's where our bananas are!"

The Kongs thanked Enguarde for his help and then swam the remaining distance to the *Gangplank Galleon*. The final battle was about to begin!

Eight

The Kongs grabbed onto a rope that hung over the *Gangplank Galleon*'s side. They pulled themselves from the water and used their natural climbing abilities to shimmy up the rope. Peering over the railing of the ship, they were shocked by what they saw.

The old ship was teeming with activity. Kremlings scurried everywhere, carrying barrels full of stolen food. As they worked, the Kremlings argued among themselves. They fought about whose turn it was to carry the barrels, whose turn it was to drop the anchor, and whose turn it was to clean the ship— although, from the look of things, it appeared that it was *never* anybody's turn to clean.

And there, in a huge pile on the deck, sat the load of stolen bananas!

The noisy, crowded ship suddenly grew silent and still. Four of the Kremlings' leaders strode onto the main deck: Klump, the helmeted Kremling who had led the raid on the banana storehouse; Rock Kroc, whose eyes glowed with evil light; Kritter, a common Kremling who had risen through the ranks by being extra-nasty; and Krusha, a huge, muscle-bound Kremling with spiked hair. Behind these four came King K. Rool, the supreme commander of the Kremlings and the one who had ordered the banana raid.

The Kongs watched this scene over the ship's railing. "That's the guy who had me put in the barrel," Diddy Kong whispered, pointing at Klump.

"It's that King K. Rool *I'd* like to get a hold of," said Donkey Kong. "He's the top Kremling."

King K. Rool addressed the crowd of Kremlings.

"My fellow Kremlings," he said. "I have just received some disturbing news. Our beloved factory has been destroyed by those meddlesome monkeys, the Kongs."

A shocked murmur passed through the crowded ship.

"Silence!" bellowed King K. Rool. "This action cannot go unpunished. Therefore, we will leave at once for a full-scale attack on the Kongs in their jungle home. This will be no banana raid. We will put an end to those mischief makers once and for all, and we will put the Kremlings in total command of Donkey Kong Island!"

A cheer went up. Donkey Kong knew they had to strike now or risk a battle that could destroy their home.

"Don't count your bananas before they're peeled, Kremlings!" shouted Donkey Kong as he, Diddy, and Cranky leapt over the ship's railing and began to fling barrels.

The attack caught the Kremlings by surprise. Donkey Kong went into a barrel roll, tumbling along the *Gangplank Galleon*'s deck like a giant hairy ball. He smashed into a group of Kremlings, scattering the startled lizards like bowling pins.

Diddy Kong vaulted high into the air and landed with a double jump right on Rock Kroc's head. The Kremling crumpled to the ground.

"Try that with me, little monkey," shouted Klump, stepping up next to Diddy. Klump smiled as he adjusted his helmet, which protected him from attacks from above.

"I don't have to," replied Diddy, "when I can do *this.*" Diddy Kong spun into a cartwheel, catching Klump in the chest with both his feet. Klump flew right over the ship's railing into the ocean.

"That's for stuffing me into a barrel!" shouted Diddy.

Meanwhile, Donkey Kong, having bowled over most of the crew with his barrel rolls, turned his attention to the Kremling commanders. He pulled out his supply of mini-barrels and began flinging them at Kritter.

Kritter made his way through the storm of barrels like an explorer fighting snow at the North Pole. "Your tiny barrels don't hurt me!" cried Kritter. Now he stood face to face with Donkey Kong.

"They don't?" said Donkey Kong. "Well, then, how about a hand-slap attack?"

Donkey Kong slammed the deck in front of Kritter with the palm of his powerful hand. The ancient wood shattered from the force of the blow, opening a huge hole right under Kritter's feet. Kritter plunged down, crashing through deck after deck. He didn't stop falling until he had reached the lowest deck of the ship.

While Donkey Kong and Diddy Kong disposed of the Kremlings, Cranky got busy loading the stolen bananas into large empty barrels.

Donkey Kong turned around and found himself face to face with Krusha, the strongest of the Kremling commanders. "Why don't you throw your little barrels at me, monkey? Ha, ha!" laughed Krusha.

"How about if I throw my big feet at you instead?" replied Donkey Kong, as he jumped right at Krusha, feet-first. Donkey Kong landed on Krusha with a tremendous blow.

Krusha just shrugged it off. "Was that a monkey or just an insect?" mocked the Kremling.

Diddy attacked from the side, cartwheeling into Krusha's powerful arms. The young monkey bounced off and landed on the deck.

"An even smaller insect this time," said Krusha. "Let me show you *real* strength." Krusha lashed out, striking Donkey Kong with one arm and Diddy with the other. The two Kongs went flying to opposite sides of the *Gangplank Galleon.*

As Krusha stood in the middle of the ship laughing, Donkey Kong and Diddy Kong realized what they had to do. They had to work together to stop this most powerful Kremling.

The two Kongs found long ropes coiled up on the sides of the ship where each had landed. They both flung ropes up over the mast and made sure they were tightly secured. Then, on the count of three, Donkey Kong and Diddy Kong swung from opposite sides of the ship toward the middle.

They met right where Krusha stood, swinging into the Kremling from two sides at once. The combination of both Kongs hitting

Krusha at once was too much even for the muscle-bound commander. Krusha fell to the deck, stunned.

"Way to go, little buddy," Donkey Kong said.

"We make a good team," replied Diddy.

"This is not over yet, though," Donkey Kong reminded him. "We've still got to stop King K. Rool!"

But the Kongs were too late. Seeing that defeat was at hand, King K. Rool had slipped away in his speedboat.

Donkey Kong and Diddy Kong watched as the supreme Kremling commander sped away from the *Gangplank Galleon*, waving his fist in the air and screaming back at them, "This isn't over, monkeys! I will be back to destroy you!" Meanwhile, the remaining Kremlings abandoned the ship rather than face the Kongs without their leaders.

Donkey Kong and Diddy soon discovered that during the battle Cranky Kong had been hard at work. Not only had he loaded all the stolen bananas into barrels, but when the barrels were full, he had lashed them together to form a giant raft.

"Nice work, Pops!" said Donkey Kong.

"This old monkey still has a trick or two up his sleeve," replied Cranky. "Besides, I wasn't about to just sit around and let you two have all the fun!"

The Kongs tossed the barrel raft over the edge, and jumped off the ship onto the raft. They paddled the raft to shore, where they loaded the bananas into the abandoned Kremling carts.

When all the bananas were safely in the carts, the Kongs began the long journey home, pulling the carts behind them. "You know," Cranky said to Donkey Kong, "for a young whippersnapper, you did a good job on this little adventure."

A warm smile broke out on Donkey Kong's face. "Thanks, Pops!" he said.

"Yeah, well, don't go all mushy on me now," said Cranky Kong.

Donkey Kong smiled again. Then he turned to Diddy. "And you, little buddy," Donkey Kong

said. "You made me proud. You can go on an adventure with me anytime!"

"Thanks, Donkey," said Diddy Kong, beaming with pride.

"You know, the Kremlings will be back," Donkey Kong added.

"And I'll give them a good thrashing again," said Cranky Kong waving his walking stick in the air.

"We'll be ready for them, Donkey," said Diddy. "We're the best team on Donkey Kong Island!"